Big Sister, I Need You

Kim Lindquist

ISBN: 9798683515409

DEDICATION

For Iris and Ida. May you find many ways to need
each other as you grow.
And for Kristen, the original Big Sister. I still need you.

Hi Big Sister! I'm here. I'll be home soon, and I've been waiting my whole life to meet you.

Big Sister, I'm home now. Mommy and Daddy have
already told me what a wonderful sister you are.

Thank you for welcoming me home Big Sister. I know very little about the world. All I know is that I need you to share Mommy and Daddy, so I can grow big and healthy and go on adventures with you.

And I know that as my Big Sister you will show me
how things work around here.

Big Sister, it's morning time, and I need you.
Can you go get Daddy for me?

Big Sister, it's nap time. I'm cranky, and I need you to show me how to rest my head and fall asleep.

Big Sister, it's lunch time. I'm hungry and I need you to show me how to be a very good eater.

Big Sister, I'm getting bigger, and I need you to show me how to play, share toys, and be gentle.

Big Sister, I'm crawling now, and I need you to show me the best routes to scoot.

Big Sister, I'm walking now, too, and I need you to teach me how to be very careful.

Big Sister, I'm learning lots every day, and I love learning from you. I need you to teach me about tickles,

and giggles,

and piggy toes, too.

Big Sister, now that I'm older, I need you to teach me about imagination!

And building forts
out of bed sheets.

And Big Sister, I need you to teach me how to ride a bike!

Big Sister, I need you to kiss
my boo-boo better, too.

And while you're at it Big Sister,

I need you to teach me about soccer

and sandcastles.

Those seem important, too.

And guess what, Big Sister? I need you to teach me about learning and going to school. Those look fun.

And Big Sister, now that we go to school together, I need you to teach me how to ride the school bus.

And I need you to teach me how to make friends, Big Sister.

And Big Sister, I need you to tell me why other kids are mean sometimes.

Big Sister, I love you.
You are such a special sister to me.

I think I'll need you as my Big Sister forever.

ABOUT THE AUTHOR

Kim Lindquist is a Little Sister with fond memories of growing up in New England with her Mom, Dad, Big Sister and dogs. Kim loves spending time with her nieces, nephews and family, especially outdoors. She lives in Boston, MA with her wonderful husband Joe and their sweet dog Wallace.

Made in United States
Troutdale, OR
01/09/2024